For Smitha, my amazing sister, who is always there for all of us,
with all my love —S. P.-H.

For all the grandparents —A. B.

Published in Great Britain in February 2016 by Bloomsbury Publishing Plc
Published in the United States of America in December 2015
by Bloomsbury Children's Books
www.bloomsbury.com

Bloomsbury is a registered trademark of Bloomsbury Publishing Plc

For information about permission to reproduce selections from this book, write to
Permissions, Bloomsbury Children's Books, 1385 Broadway, New York, New York 10018
Bloomsbury books may be purchased for business or promotional use. For information on bulk purchases please contact
Macmillan Corporate and Premium Sales Department at specialmarkets@macmillan.com

Inspired by Isaiah 41:10 & 43:1–3

Library of Congress Cataloging-in-Publication Data
available upon request
ISBN 978-1-61963-922-5 (hardcover)
ISBN 978-1-61963-923-2 (e-book) • ISBN 978-1-61963-924-9 (e-PDF)

Art created with acrylic paint and colored pencil • Typeset in Horley Old Style • Book design by Kristina Coates

Printed in the U.S.A. by Worzalla, Stevens Point, Wisconsin
4 6 8 10 9 7 5 3

Smriti Prasadam-Halls

illustrated by Alison Brown

I'll
Never
Let You
Go

BLOOMSBURY

NEW YORK   LONDON   OXFORD   NEW DELHI   SYDNEY

When you are happy,
I hear you sing . . .

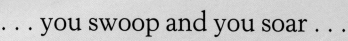

. . . you swoop and you soar . . .

you LOVE everything.

When you are naughty, I see that, too . . .

But I know that *really* you know what to do.

When you are bothered and all in a flap,
I wait by your side while you snip and you snap.

When you're excited, the world joins with you.

You bounce all about—look, I'm bouncing, too!

When you are sad and troubled with fears,
I hold you close and dry all your tears.

When you are sleeping, curled up so tight,
I stay awake, keeping watch through the night.

When you are quiet, I think with you.

I help you find answers, work out what to do.

When you are brave, I'm at your side,
and every adventure we'll take in our stride.

When you aren't sure, you'll feel me near.
When you are scared, I will be here.

For when you are high and when you are low,

I'll be holding you tight . . .

. . . and I'll never let go.